T0131922

To order additional copies of this book, contact:
Xlibris
844-714-8691
www.Xlibris.com
Orders@Xlibris.com

ISBN: 978-1-6641-4024-0 (sc)
ISBN: 978-1-6641-4025-7 (hc)
ISBN: 978-1-6641-4023-3 (e)

Print information available on the last page

Rev. date: 11/06/2020

ROBERT FINDS HIS SPACE

By Jean Edwards

Illustrations by
Jean Edwards

Robert was the youngest in his family. He could not catch up. His brother and sisters were all older and they knew more about everything. Robert tried to do all the things they did, but he could not catch up. He became very discouraged.

It was winter, but there was no snow to make a snowman, or even for sledding with his dog, Texas. Also, the pond wasn't frozen hard enough for skating.

One day in December, he was looking at the fireplace and thinking about Santa coming down the chimney at Christmas, and he got an idea. If Santa could go around the world in space and then come down the chimney, why couldn't he go up? He made up his mind to do it.

First, he would need some equipment....
a helmet so his head wouldn't bang
on the bricks going up the chimney,
and a warm suit, because it would
be cold in outer space.

Looking in the toy box he found his football helmet and he decided it was perfect, but the space suit was a bigger problem. Hunting through the bureau drawers in his bedroom he found his one piece suit of long underwear. He tried it on with the helmet and he was pleased with the effect of the outfit.

He ran to the kitchen where he made a peanut butter sandwich and wrapped it in plastic wrap, then put it in the leather pouch he called his Indian Bag, just in case he was late for supper.

"This is going to be a swell trip," he thought to himself, as he collected pillows from the couch and put them in the empty fireplace. It was a little sooty, but Robert never minded a little dirt. He arranged his pillows and nestled down in them to prepare for take-off.

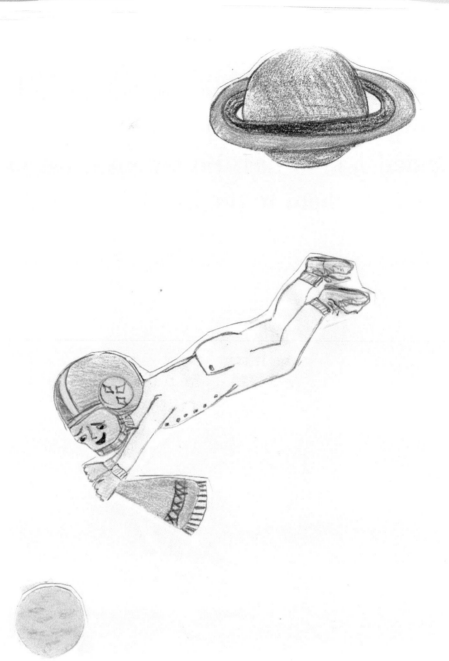

He was thinking and thinking about how he would launch himself, when suddnely "WOOSH" up the chimney he went - up over the housetops, up through the clouds, heading straight for the moon. Robert burst out laughing. At last he was doing something his brother and sisters had never even thought of doing. He decided not to stop on the moon, someone had already been there.

Perhaps he would go to Saturn, with all the pretty rings around it, or maybe Pluto, so he could tell everyone he had been to Pluto. Then he changed his mind, because some of his friends might laugh and say, "Yes, Pluto, the dog with long ears." He remembered how they had laughed when he ate raw carrots every day when he wanted to grow big ears like a rabbit. Not only was it a big disappointment, it became a family joke.

No, he would go to Jupiter, the biggest planet in the solar system! But then, someone might make funny stories about him jumping to Jupiter, and he didn't want anyone saying "Jumping Jupiter!" when they saw him jumping on his pogo stick.

One had to be careful making choices. Finally he found himself heading straight for Mars. That's it! Mars! Everyone says there might be life on Mars and now he could find out for sure!

Jumping down from the sky of Mars, Robert landed near a big ocean and there on the muddy beach he saw little bubbles in the sand. He found a stick and dug in the wet sand until he came up with a clam. Hoorah!! Proof at last, of one of his greatest adventures!

He put the clam in with the peanut butter sandwich and suddenly felt very tired. "This space travel is hard work," he thought. He nestled down by a big rock and "POOF!" suddenly he was back in his chimney launch pad at home. He reached into his Indian Bag and all he could find was his peanut butter sandwich. The clam was gone!!

He had lost it on the way back from Mars. That was all right, but without proof Robert decided not to tell anyone about his great adventure. He would go again someday, now that he knew he could do it, and then he would become famous, but for now he would eat his peanut butter sandwich and go out and ride his bike.

It was good to know he had been someplace and done something strange and wonderful and he would not have to worry about catching up anymore.

Robert had found his space!

Printed in the United States
By Bookmasters